Never Nothing

Blame the Tide

Table of Contents

CHAPTER ONE 1

CHAPTER TWO...13

CHAPTER THREE.. 37

CHAPTER FOUR.. 59

CHAPTER FIVE.. 69

CHAPTER SIX 91

CHAPTER ONE

Bancroft Manor

With the servants in Eagle Rock for the weekend, Hank took it upon himself to cook breakfast for his sons. Normally they would go to a restaurant on Saturday mornings, but with the recent media circus and Floyd's new unwillingness to go out in public, the whole tradition was suddenly now more of a massive burden than anything else.

Floyd hadn't willingly spoken to his dad since his release from the hospital, and secretly Hank was glad for it. Not that he would ever admit it, of course; but if Floyd wasn't talking, it meant he also wasn't complaining or being insolent. Theo wasn't saying much, either, but that was okay, too. Hank desperately needed the peace and quiet.

Hank didn't bother to wake up his oldest for breakfast. He knew the moment he threw the bacon on that Floyd would rise up like a cartoon and follow his nose down the stairs. Theo was seated at the table, reading a comic book, when Hank's phone rang. Since Daven and Rupert were still blocked, there was really only one person who would be calling him at a time like this. Well, maybe two, but he already knew which one it was.

"Hey Taylor."

"Good morning, boss. I just got a call on the emergency line from an anonymous agent."

Hank turned off the stove and removed all the pans. "Hang on." Then, to Theo, "I'll be right back. Make sure the dogs don't jump up on the counter to get at the food."

He went into his study and locked the door.

"God, I'm afraid to ask. What's going on?"

"As soon as I answered he blurted out that he was the one who called Daven on Christmas eve and Rupert on Christmas day. He won't speak to anyone but you and said he will call in exactly 48 hours. That is literally all he told me, verbatim. I didn't get a word in edgewise before he hung up."

Taylor sounded scared, and Hank knew why. She didn't want to be accused of talking with an unverified asset, like her unfortunate colleagues.

"It's okay. You did good. Speaking of which, I didn't get the chance to ask you yesterday if there is any news about those meetings I had before Christmas? Any clue as to who could have been the secret Urbane?"

Taylor sighed a little. "Well, I've been able to definitely exclude three of them, and I'm focusing on the other two. I promise you I will have a better update on Monday evening."

"Can you come to my new house on Monday morning at 7 for this call? I'll call you tomorrow with the address and gate code."

"Will do. See you then."

Hank's heart was pounding so hard that he felt physically ill and had to sit down for a few minutes. Normally at a time like this he would be rapidly dialing Daven to get his take on the incident, but that was the farthest thing from his mind right now.

He picked up his phone and scrolled through his work emails, then took a peek into his personal email, which was nearly all junk. But there was one message from Rupert's personal email that was two days old.

"Hank, just wanted to let you know Dav and I are going to Maui for a week. Back on January 6. Happy New Year."

Rupert had a little beach house there. It would do both of them a lot of good to get away and have some privacy, so Hank was happy for them, but he still deleted the message without responding. By the time he returned to the kitchen, Floyd was hovering over the bacon and the dogs had been taken outside, where they were busy struggling for custody of a Frisbee, tails banging against the French doors.

"Floyd, sit down. Bacon's not done yet."

"Yes, sir." Floyd turned and sat, then picked up one of Theo's comic books.

"How's your stomach?"

"Fine, sir."

Again with the unnecessary *sir*. Hank resisted a sigh as he pulled the pan back on the stove.

"Theody, why don't you go play with the dogs for a minute. I want to talk to your brother."

"Yeah, right. You guys just want to eat all the bacon for yourselves!"

Hank scowled. "I'm hurt. That's not true. You know we'll save a couple slices for the dogs."

"You suck, dad." Theo grinned and went outside, where he joined in the struggle for the Frisbee.

Hank said absolutely nothing in a test to see what Floyd would do. Sure enough, the boy began fidgeting as he waited for his dad to speak. Then he started drumming the table, which he knew his dad hated. Hank didn't take the bait.

A few minutes passed, and Floyd couldn't take it anymore. Just what Hank was hoping for.

"What is it, dad?"

Hank smiled a little. "Oh good, I'm *dad* again. Thought you disowned me there for a while. Food's done, go get your brother."

Floyd blinked, expecting to have a little more of a talk than just that. Hank turned away and busied himself with the dishes.

Urbane HQ - Denver

Harmon normally didn't work on Saturdays, much less on New Year's eve, but it was a new era. Colbert was obsessed with the idea that Janet had been a double agent, and now Harmon was convinced, too. The possibility was driving him crazy. Her murder had been planned to frame Hank, but now everything could be turned upside down. He wasn't the praying type, but if he was, he would have been asking for the tapes to not show even the slightest glimpse of Yannick.

Colbert was also convinced that Yannick didn't realize he was on Seditionists property at the time. Harmon wasn't so sure. The man had turned before, and could turn again. In fact, considering they hadn't heard from him in a week, that was increasingly becoming a possibility, too.

Harmon took another drink of chai tea and flipped through the final pages of the charter. He had chosen to write that one out first, since it was shortest, but it was still taking far too long. Damn Stewart and his schoolboy punishments.

Colbert walked into his office without a sound, as usual.

"Boss? Got a second?"

"Yeah. Sit down."

Colbert's massive body made the chair creak. "I was wondering...I hope you don't mind me bringing this up again. But I thought you were going to ask Bancroft if Janet was a double agent? You've spoken to him twice since we agreed on that, and-"

"Yeah, I know. But he's not going to tell us if she is. Or was, rather."

"Still might be good to ask. We might be able to figure it out from his reaction."

Harmon set down his pen and leaned back. "Look, I've been thinking. One more misstep and I'm out. You understand that, right?"

Colbert nodded. "Yes."

"So...I'm all but praying the FBI doesn't identify Yannick. If they do, Hank will reveal Janet was double and then it will make even less sense that she was killed by one of their own agents on their own property. And *then* it will become clear that Yannick was also double. Then I'm out of the game. So we're going to leave this Janet issue alone right now and wait for the FBI to hopefully declare it a cold case. So don't ask me again, please. In fact, don't even mention her at all."

Colbert was stone-faced. "I understand. So that brings up just one more question, and then I'll shut up. May I? Thank you. I have a feeling Bancroft set you up with that press conference of his. He wanted you to take the bait."

"I know, we've already discussed this. I was stupid and I'm paying the price."

"Okay. Sorry. My point is, he wanted you exactly where you are now, and he got it. Which means she was double. Period. What makes you think Hank won't volunteer that information himself?"

"Because he doesn't know what side the killer was on. Are we done now?"

"Yes. That's the last time I'll mention it."

Harmon took a deep breath and calmed down a little. "I actually happen to agree with you, which is why I'm walking the straight and narrow from here on out. It's time for me to accept I can't win against Hank Bancroft. Never have before, and he's getting smarter every time. There's no reason we can't just start cooperating with him. It's not like our parties are that different."

Colbert was incensed. "Cooperating? You can't be serious."

"I am. At least on the subjects we happen to agree with. The government is really our biggest enemy right now, Colbert. Look at what they're doing with trying to strengthen the felony manual labor laws. It's slowly escalating to cruel and unusual punishment over the years. We've watched it happening and done nothing, because we're too proud to band together and fight back. And that's just one example of where we should be cooperating."

"You're basically talking about rebelling against the government."

"No. It's called lobbying. We would never be doing anything illegal. Speaking of which, if Yannick ever calls back, tell him his services are no longer needed and we'll send him a nice payment for what he's done so far. In fact, why don't you try calling him again today and letting him know."

"I doubt we'll ever hear from him again," muttered Colbert.

"Fine with me. What he apparently did to Daven and Rupert is more than satisfying enough. But I'm telling you, as of right now, this subterfuge stops. I don't want to lose my job. We have to focus on other things from here on out. And you know there's another reason I want to work with Hank."

Colbert smiled. "Ah yes, I wondered when you would quote Napoleon again. It's been at least two days. *Keep your friends close, and your enemies closer* ."

Harmon smiled back as he stood up. "Exactly. Here, I'll get some cash out of the safe for Yannick in order to entice him to meet you. Then let him know outright he is never to contact us again or we'll turn him in for his little cocaine trafficking side job."

"You got it, boss. He'll want to see a payment slip to know this isn't a trick. I won't actually give it to him, of course."

"No problem. Fill it out for me and I'll sign it."

"Yannick? It's Colbert."

"What's all that noise?" Yannick asked.

"Just wind. Sorry, I'm driving and the sunroof is open. Hang
on." There was a long mechanical sound as the roof closed.
"Listen, I just left Harmon's office. He wanted me to pass
along a message to you."

"Oh great. What now?"

"He's really happy about the work you did with Daven and
Rupert. Wants to send you a nice big payment for it, and an
advance for other future services which I'm about to ask you
for."

"What services?"

"Among other things, he wants you to call the FBI and tell
them you were ordered by Hank Bancroft to kill Janet, because
he no longer trusted her as a double agent. With the hope that
in doing so on Seditionists property, Harmon would be
framed. Obviously you'll have to use a voice changer and

everything. I have some other details to share first before you do that, so they know you are legit."

Another long pause from Yannick. "Okay. I'll need authorization from Harmon directly, as you know."

"I have it right here, and the payment as well. In cash."

"Cash?"

'Yes, indeed. Where can we meet?"

CHAPTER TWO

Bancroft Manor

Hank slammed his hand down on the alarm clock and turned over with a grumble. Today was the day their mystery man was due to call, and Taylor was due to the house in an hour. He almost didn't want to know what the strange caller had to say, and the overwhelming desire to quit his job and go live in a cabin in the woods overtook him for the tenth time since Christmas, at least. Nothing really seemed worth living under such stress anymore.

He fell back asleep and was soon awakened by the second alarm that had been set for 6:30am.

La Quinta Inn, Phoenix Airport

Yannick once again opened his wallet and counted the money advance that Colbert had given him to frame Hank Bancroft for Janet's murder. He smiled, and then counted it once more. For this kind of cash, he'd do pretty much anything.

He picked up the phone in his room, connected the voice changer to the mouthpiece, and dialed Stewart in Philadelphia.

FBI Headquarters, Philadelphia

"This is Stewart, how may I help you?"

"Uh, yes. I'm calling in with an anonymous tip in the case of the recent murder in Colorado."

Stewart sat straight up. "I'm listening. Please proceed."

"I'm going to give it to you straight, then I'm hanging up before you can trace me. I'm a professional hit man. Hank Bancroft contacted me and offered me $10,000 cash to kill Janet. I declined, but obviously he got someone else to agree to it."

"I see. And did he give you a reason for wanting to kill her?"

"Yes. He said she's a double agent for the Seditionists, and that I was to follow her to a drop-off spot on their property so that Harmon would be blamed once Bancroft announced she was double. He wanted me to shoot her in the back of the head with an untraceable bullet, which I wouldn't have been able to obtain in time. Hence, my reason for declining."

"Okay. Why are you turning him in and taking the risk of being identified? Your motives for calling me are just as important as Bancroft's are for killing Janet. For example, maybe someone paid you even more money to pin the blame on him."

Yannick hadn't expected that question, but he was a smooth talker and a fast thinker. "If I'm not telling the truth, how could I possibly know she was a double agent, or the details of her execution method? Goodbye, Stewart. Time to do your job and lock him up."

Maui, Hawaii

"Dav...it's almost 4 o'clock in the morning. What are doing out here sitting in the dark?"

"I don't know. Can't sleep. Why are you awake?"

Rupert shrugged in the dark, even knowing the other man couldn't see the gesture. "Same deal, I guess." He sat down, too. "Can't stop wondering if Hank will ever forgive us."

"Well, stop wondering. He won't. My brain is actually stuck on those calls we got on the emergency line. Do you think he's doing anything at all to identify that person?"

"No, but Taylor is. She started working on that before we got...in trouble. All I know is that part of me still believes he was telling the truth, that Hank unknowingly met with an Urbane and paid out money to get something done. He's done similar things before, although none of it has ever been against the law."

Daven sighed. "You mean like the time he paid off Floyd's teacher to tutor him at his house in order to prevent him from repeating 8th grade? Or paid a reporter to destroy camera film on the spot? Things like that?"

"Yeah. Like I said, not against the law, and hardly scandalous."

"No, but not exactly kosher, either. He's done some really borderline shady things. I don't like how he flaunts his ability to charm his way out of trouble. Or the way he plans moves way in advance like a chess master, and I'm referring to the whole thing with Harmon and the FBI tapes. That is a case study in Machiavellian strategy. I know he's never technically broken the law, but Rupe...he's going to cross the line someday, if he hasn't already. It's inevitable. He thinks he's untouchable."

Rupe laughed a little. "Daven, you've known him for over ten years and you're just now realizing this? I knew that from day one. Come on."

Daven shook his head. "No, I knew. But recently...well, he's gone from merely playing with fire to actually burning himself on purpose with that press conference stunt, and I swear to god he enjoyed every second of the smoldering wreckage he left behind. I've never seen him do anything like that before. Have you?"

"No. But he's had a very long rivalry with Harmon, and maybe it just feels good to see the man put in his place for once."

"For *once* ? Hank forced him into a final warning with the president, and he was also the cause of all three warnings before that. He's going to get taken out just like Janet if he's not careful, or maybe locked up, and then his sons...you know what, I'm sorry I brought it up."

"Seriously, Dav? That's what I'm here for. To talk these things out. I'm just trying to play the devil's advocate here."

Daven grumbled, "You're doing a shitty job by just defending him blindly. Don't you realize how self-destructive and dangerous he's become lately? I can't be the only one seeing this. His ego is going to be his downfall, and disaster is just around the corner.'

Rupert said nothing for a long time.

"You still awake?" Dav prompted after a while.

"Yeah. Just thinking about all you've said. Dav, you've never doubted him until we got that call. Never. Did it really rattle you that much? Don't you think it could just easily be something Harmon set up in order to shake our confidence? Hank isn't the only chess master in this game, you know. None of our agents in their right minds would ever refuse to give their identifying code. The only thing that stands to reason is that he wasn't one of our agents at all."

Daven was quiet for a little while, and then he replied, "No, actually. I hadn't given that much thought."

"Well maybe you should, before you keep excoriating Hank any further. Maybe he isn't the only one who is getting exactly what he wants right now. If anything, Harmon is more dangerous now because he's cunning *and* desperate not to let Hank win again. I'd be willing to bet big bucks that Hank is going to step aside entirely at this point and just wait for Harmon to fall on his own sword."

"Yeah. I see what you mean. Thanks, Rupe."

"Sure. Go back to bed. This will all be clearer in the morning."

"God, I hope so."

Bancroft Manor

Taylor's phone rang at exactly 8am, and even though Hank was expecting it, he still nearly had a coronary when it happened.

"Hank Bancroft."

"Mr. Bancroft. I'm using a voice changer, so don't try to identify me."

"Fine. What do you want?"

"I am the person who called Daven on Christmas eve and claimed you met with an Urbane and gave him money to plant an agent in the government."

"Okay. And who are you, exactly?"

"I'm calling to tell you it was someone higher up in your own party who put me up to it. Not Rupert or Daven. But someone within your headquarters."

"I see. And you're an Urbane yourself, I gather?"

"I was, yes. Now I'm neither party. You're all really fucked up, you know that?"

Hank cleared his throat, not sure what to say next. Taylor looked at him and shrugged, her face a picture of blank confusion.

"Right, so...why are you calling to tell me this, exactly?"

"Simple. My loyalties lie to my bank account now, so I want you to pay me a lot of money to tell you who it was that put me up to this. I'll call you back in exactly 7 days from now to hear your initial offer. Expect to negotiate up for a while. Goodbye."

"Wait-"

The line went dead, and Hank wasn't really sure if his heart was still beating or not.

La Quinta Inn, Phoenix Airport

Yannick hung up the phone and grabbed his duffel to make his way to the airport. While he waited at the gate, he made a quick call to Colbert.

"Hello, kind sir. Stewart is aware of the situation. Vacation's over and I'm headed back to Los Angeles now for my drudgery of a day job. Awaiting further instructions....and payment."

Colbert laughed. "Who knew a mere accounts payable specialist could be so treacherous."

"Oh, my friend. I have not yet begun to fight. Just you wait. Talk soon."

Yannick hung up, and then smiled as he pulled out his Seditionists employee ID badge and studied his picture for the hundredth time. Almost five years at the company now, just enough to avoid suspicion. He wasn't sure how long he could play both sides, but it sure was going to be fun while it lasted. And quite profitable, if the past two days were any indication.

January 9

Hank was fitfully resting in bed after the Sunday servants banquet while one of his dreaded tension headaches pounded like a bass drum on his temples. This was disappointing considering it had been an unusually peaceful week, with both of his boys behaving perfectly and the paparazzi mostly leaving them alone. The latter was mostly because business was back to where it had basically been before Christmas, with no new inflammatory press releases or devastating news to report. Even Harmon was being nice on their daily calls, saying nothing that raised Hank's hackles or gave him reason for suspicion. Taylor was still working diligently on all her leads, and Hank was confident they would have an answer to his many questions soon.

He already knew he wasn't going to offer the mystery caller any money, so that point of stress was on the side burner for now. If there really was a mole in the company, which he doubted, he would ask for Daven's help to sniff him or her out. In the meantime, he had to focus on his own overwhelming workload.

Hank was just about doze off, but groaned as his phone began buzzing on the dresser. He would have given anything to be able to ignore it with no damage to his conscience.

"Yeah, Avery. What's up?"

"Boss, sorry to be the bearer of bad news. Your sons just got kicked out of the library."

"Oh god," Hank moaned. "I knew this day was too good to be true. What exactly did they do?"

Avery continued, "They were scuffling. One of them - they won't say who - knocked over a sculpture and broke it. Shattered it, actually. I'm being asked to pay for it on the spot."

Hank closed his eyes and counted to ten in order to compose himself. Boys will be boys, and he had been just as much of a delinquent at that age...but his father wasn't constantly in the spotlight, either. Floyd and Theo knew better than to draw negative attention to themselves, and that's what infuriated him.

"Okay. I hope it's not some kind of Ming Dynasty vase."

"No, but they're asking for almost three thousand dollars, sir."

Hank pinched the bridge of his nose. "And my sons were definitely at fault?"

"Yes, sir. I saw part of it happen, just not enough to conclude which one of them did it."

"Okay. Put whoever is asking you for money on the phone with me, please."

Another pause, some shuffling noise. "This is Tami."

"Good morning, ma'am. This is the father of the boys who broke your sculpture. I'm so very sorry. Will you please give Avery a bill for my records? I'll have him return with payment in the morning."

Her tone was highly skeptical. *"Right.* You'll just voluntarily return with a few thousand dollars sometime tomorrow. I'll just call the police and make a report, instead. Thank you anyway."

"Wait." Hank realized with a start that this woman didn't know who the boys were, or who he was. That could be a good thing about 99% of the time, but right now it was pretty much the worst thing. "Ma'am, make out the bill now and I'll be over in twenty minutes with cash. Yes, *cash* . My boys will stay there with their, er, babysitter until I get there. Please don't call the police. You'll understand why when I arrive."

There was a pause long enough to make Hank worry, but then she finally agreed. "Twenty minutes, then. That's all I'm giving you. We close in half an hour," she added firmly.

"Thank you, ma'am."

Hank cussed up a storm as he spun the dial to his safe and pulled out the cash, but his sense of humored returned quickly when he pulled up fifteen minutes later in the Thunderbird with Vance; Tami turned sheet white and grasped onto Avery to keep herself upright.

"Mr. Bancroft. *I'm so, so sorry.* I didn't know that was you."

Hank struggled not laugh at Avery's expression as he pretended to be contrite. "Please accept my apologies for not introducing myself. May I have the bill?"

She handed it over with a shaky hand, eying him like he was a lion about to take down a gazelle. "Do you...I mean, want the evidence, and your boys said they did it, and...if I would have known-"

"Ma'am, it's okay. I promise I don't bite." He pulled open his wallet and pulled out $2,940. "I'd like a receipt, please. As quick as you can. And discreetly, if you don't mind."

"Of course, sir."

Hank walked away and climbed into the SUV where Theo and Floyd were waiting, slamming the door behind him. Avery stayed outside with Vance and moved away to the other side.

"It was me, dad," Theo confessed immediately. "I bumped into it."

Hank was surprised to find he couldn't muster up any real anger about the incident. On the contrary, he felt deeply sorry for his sons. They couldn't get into any kind of trouble without the threat of it being all over the news the next day, and that wasn't fair. Hardly a childhood at all.

But it wouldn't do to let his children think they could act like hooligans just because their father felt guilty for being a public figure. He cleared his throat and affected an angry expression.

"*Bumped* into it. While doing what? Having a seizure?"

Theo swallowed hard. "No. We were, I was...well, it just kind of happened."

"It was my fault," put in Floyd, very quietly.

Hank resisted the urge to ask them no further questions and forgive them on the spot. They wouldn't learn anything that way.

"Rough housing in the library, huh? Are you trying to get yourselves-"

Theo protested immediately, "Dad, we weren't rough housing. Floyd had a panic attack-"

"Shut up, Theody!" hissed Floyd.

"You shut up*!"*

"Boys!" yelled Hank. "What the hell? Theo, finish your explanation. Floyd, shut it or else."

Theo was breathing hard. "He *was* having a panic attack, and he kind of shoved me backwards trying to get outside, and I fell into the pedestal that the sculpture was on. It wasn't his fault, he just needed to get some air and he was freaking out."

Floyd was instantly irate. "No I wasn't! We were fighting because Theo was being obnoxious."

"I was not! You were totally freaking the fuck out over nothing!"

"It wasn't nothing!" Floyd objected.

"I was trying to *help* you, you stupid piece of-"

Floyd shoved his brother backwards and Theo shoved back even harder, then they started hitting each other. Hank separated them easily by dragging Theo over his lap on the opposite side of the car.

"Alright, that's settled. You're both getting punished when we get home. You'll go directly to my study-"

"I didn't do anything!" protested Theo angrily, at same time Floyd said, "It was an accident!"

Now Hank's anger was real. "I don't care about the sculpture! The world will be fine with one less crappy piece of art. But I will not abide you being dishonest with your guards and fighting each other, period, and by that I'm referring to what just happened in this car. You know better than that."

They did, too, and they finally settled down with matching guilty expressions.

"Sorry. Do we have to pay you back the three thousand, dad?" Theo asked nervously.

"No. You're both getting paddled after you apologize to Avery, and that will be the end of it. Floyd, are you okay?" asked Hank after a moment, when it appeared his oldest had completely tuned out and was in his own world again.

Floyd didn't look up. "I'm sorry, sir," he said miserably.

"What caused you to panic?"

"I didn't panic."

Theo answered for him. "There was a guy following us around and taking pictures."

"What? *Inside* the library, you mean?"

"No, outside. He was stalking us through the windows."

Hank was not surprised to hear this at all. Goddamned paparazzi.

"Floyd, I'm going to ask you one last time. Are you ok now, or not? Theo, you be quiet."

"No, dad. I'm not okay. I'm a freakin' basket case and you know it."

Damn it. "Alright. So you did panic. It's okay. Anything you need from me before we head home?"

Floyd shrugged yet again, almost appearing not to answer. But then he blurted out angrily, "For the hundredth time, I need you to quit your fucking job! Then I wouldn't have to deal with this shit in the first place."

Hank flinched and nearly snapped back, but managed to keep his cool.

"Hop out of the car, Theo, and get in with Vance. Have him take you home."

"Yes, sir," responded Theo with a stunned expression as he climbed out.

"Yeah, go home and cry to your stuffed animals, Theody," Floyd muttered.

"*Floyd!*" Hank softened his tone and looked down at his anxious youngest son. "We'll talk later. Go."

Theo nodded, chin quivering, as he turned away.

"I want to go home now," Floyd said quietly, still not looking at his father.

"We're going. Just waiting on a receipt. Did you take your anxiety medicine today?"

Floyd nodded. "Yes, sir."

"Okay. Listen up. I've made a decision. You're going to counseling, and no amount of protesting is going to make me change my mind. So don't start. And I'm going to ask Rupert if you and Theo can home school with his kids. It will take you out of the spotlight a little. We've talked about it before, and you didn't seem against the idea."

"I'm not against it at all," Floyd replied. There was nothing he wanted more, actually, and it upset him that he wasn't already homeschooled. "You should know that considering I've asked you about it a million times, but you never listen because you don't care."

"Settle down, Floyd," Hank replied mildly, hoping Floyd would shut the hell up before he took things too far.

"It's true. You never listen to me and only pretend to care how I feel. Theo doesn't care, either. The only person who is always nice to me is Uncle Dav. Forget home school, I want to go back to boarding school so I don't have to put up with this shit."

"If you don't calm down immediately, we're going to have a problem."

"You're already the problem, dad!"

Floyd suddenly burst into tears, and Hank got out of the car in disgust. Tami was just starting to walk back towards the group, and he waited patiently for her to reach him and hand him the receipt.

"Here you go, sir. Again, I'm so very sorry for what I said on the phone."

"Who was the artist of the piece they broke?" Hank asked out of curiosity.

"The original founder of the library, actually. He died last year."

Hank felt extra horrible all of a sudden. "Oh, shit. I mean...forgive me. I can't express how sorry I am. When I return home I'll make a donation to the library in his memory."

"That would be nice. Thank you."

"Sure. Uh. Have a good evening if you can, I guess?" He cringed at his own awkwardness. "I'm sorry. I mean well."

"I know," Tami replied with a thin smile. "Your sons are still being banished from our library for one year, though. Have a good evening, too...if you can." She winked flirtatiously, gave a little shimmy, and then walked away.

Hank blanched, then glanced aside at Avery, who was clearly shocked as well, but in an entirely different way altogether.

"Don't you dare laugh," he muttered out of the corner of his mouth as they stared at the departing woman. "I will kill you where you stand, I swear it."

"Might be worth it, boss," he replied dryly.

Vance had gotten back into the car abruptly and was all but writhing in silent hysterics.

"Traitors, the lot of you," Hank declared with good humor as he turned away. "Let's go."

"Dad," blurted Floyd as his father reappeared in the SUV. "I didn't mean what I said."

"We'll talk later." Floyd nodded and went quiet, so Hank looked at Avery through the rearview mirror as the man got in the car and shut the door. His eyes were sparkling.

"You alright there, Chief?"

There was a strangled chuckle, and then a gravely formal reply. "Yes, sir, I'm fine. Home?" he asked.

"No. Let's stop by Daven's house. But first pull through the Shake Shack so I can use the restroom and Floyd can get some food."

Shake Shack

"Good afternoon, Hank," answered a very surprised Daven. Hank hadn't called him in almost two weeks, and Dav was starting to think he never would hear from him again.

"Are you home?"

"Yes...you called me on my house phone, remember?"

Hank was in a locked restroom by himself, but he still lowered his voice almost to a whisper. "Right, sorry. Floyd really wants to see you. We had a bit of a blowup today. I feel extremely awkward asking, but if you don't have any plans, can he come over for a bit and play with Shannon?"

"Yes. You shouldn't feel awkward, Hank. He's been over here plenty of times before. May I ask what the blowup was about, so I'm prepared in case he mentions it?"

"No, it's best if I don't say anything. Let's just say he's finally entered his *I hate you* stage, so...it's been rough."

"I see. Well, I'm here, so whenever you want to send him over. I don't really have any food for him or anything though, haven't been to the store in a while."

"That's okay. We'll drop him off. I'm ten minutes away. Thanks, Dav. I owe you."

CHAPTER THREE

Daven's House

Daven was waiting outside when Avery pulled up the drive. There were, surprisingly, no cars out front at all, which meant the press had become tired of waiting for something exciting to happen at the Johansson house. So Floyd quickly jumped out, excited to hear Shannon barking madly from inside the house. He hugged Daven briefly and then ran inside.

Hank hadn't been planning to get out of the car, but Floyd had left all the food behind, so other than asking Avery to do it there was no other choice. He grabbed everything and climbed up to the porch.

"Hey," he said, somewhat shyly, unsure of what else to say, and it wasn't because he was upset or anything. It's just that Dav was wearing a very nice suit and looked as though he'd been at some kind of professional function. *Or a job interview.* And Hank didn't want to give away that it was the very first thing he noticed.

"Nice to see you, Hank." He looked over to the car and nodded with a slight smile at Avery. "I was upstairs in the balcony at church with Rupert this morning. We didn't want to disturb you."

"Oh, good. So now I don't have to yell at you guys for not going. Um." He handed the bags over and the tray of drinks. "You said you didn't have food, so we got your favorite burger with onion rings. And a root beer float, of course."

"Oh." Daven looked puzzled as he took the tray and drinks. "That's....really nice. Thank you. Can you open the door for me, please?"

Hank opened the screen with one hand and the front door with the other, but stayed on the porch. Daven did not invite him in, for which he was grateful. The last thing he needed right now was more awkwardness.

After setting everything down in the kitchen, Dav came back to the front door. "Thanks so much, Hank. That was thoughtful. How long do you want him to stay? He's already out in the backyard throwing Shannon's Frisbee. Seems very cheerful."

"Yeah, well that's because he's away from me. I really appreciate this and I'll make sure he doesn't overstay his welcome. Just kind of discreetly call me when you're ready for him to leave."

"I can't," Daven replied evenly. "You blocked my numbers."

Hank flushed. "Ah. Right. Um." He took his phone out. "Let me fix that." He scrolled through the settings for a few long awkward moments before realizing he had no clue how to unblock a contact. Daven realized it shortly after he did and held his hand out.

"Here, I'll do it." He took the proffered phone and quickly completed the task without any trouble, then handed it back.

"I have to leave for dinner in two hours, but that should be long enough. Shannon gets exhausted pretty quickly at her age."

"Right, um...where's your guard?" Hank had noticed the little BMW wasn't in the driveway.

"I gave him the week off."

"Without a replacement? You can't do that, Dav. You should *never* be without a guard. We've talked about this before, about how it blatantly violates our security policies."

"Well," said Daven with a small smile as his eyes swept up and down the street. The very empty street. "It's not like I have anyone after me right now."

Hank tried to ignore the simmering anger that suddenly overtook him. "I don't care. You're getting another guard and that's the end of it. I'm sending Lucas over as a substitute, and you're going to take him everywhere with you. This isn't negotiable."

"Very well." Daven wasn't smiling now, but he didn't protest. After all, with Floyd in his house he should damned well have a guard standing by. Hank called Lucas, who said he would be over in two minutes.

"How was Maui?" Hank asked abruptly as he hung up the phone, trying to shake off his all-too familiar irritation with Daven's disregard for his own safety.

"I wouldn't mind spending more time there, let's just put it that way."

"Hmmm. Rupert comes back to work Tuesday, as you know."

"Yes."

"I..." Hank hesitated, not wanting to force Daven into a conversation he didn't want. But he was desperate for someone to talk to. "Look, I, umm..."

"Come inside, Hank," Dav said abruptly as he turned away.

"No, I don't want-"

"Hank," repeated Daven with more urgency. "Come inside. *Now,* if you don't mind."

Hank was puzzled at first, but then he turned to follow Daven's glance down the street.

"Oh, fuck. Really?" The press were coming; Hank and Dav knew the cars anywhere. It was always the same group who arrived first on a scene, and within seconds the four cars were lined up across the street with telephoto lenses at the ready. The screened-in porch wasn't enough to completely block them, so Hank went in and closed the door behind him.

"God, I'm sorry. Thought we got away from them at the drive thru."

"It's alright. They were following Lucas, I think." Daven waited a minute and then stepped back outside to unlock the screen door and let the man in. He nodded and then silently started to make his rounds about the house, keeping one eye out the front windows all the time.

Daven had the news running in the background in the living room, and Hank happened to glance at it out of the corner of his eye and saw a very familiar sight. Sure enough, it was live video from somewhere outside Daven's house. He dashed over to the remote and turned up the volume.

"-question of what happens when Rupert Aster returns to work Tuesday, and whether or not the trust can ever be regained between them. As you can see, Hank Bancroft clearly doesn't hold too much of a grudge against Mr. Johansson, at whose house he arrived with his son a short time ago after stopping first at the Shake Shack on Pico and Westwood for some burgers and root beer floats, just in time to watch the big game. We'll stay on the scene and go live again when we obtain more information about their dramatic incident at the library only an hour ago-"

Hank muted it angrily as the unexciting footage of him entering the house with bags of food was shown, and then shown yet again.

Daven looked at him askance. *"Dramatic incident at the library ..?"*

"Fuck. There are cameras hidden in the trees outside your house. Probably at mine, too. I'm starting to get why Floyd is having a meltdown every day over this shit." He sat down on the couch and grabbed his float, inhaling almost all of it in one fell swoop before he realized he was making himself at home way too easily. He jumped to his feet.

"I'm sorry, Dav. I...it's been a day. Can I sit for a minute?"

"Of course. Eat, please. At the table though, if you don't mind."

At that moment Floyd came bouncing in through the sliding glass door, Shannon close on his heels. "Uncle Dav, the Frisbee is stuck on the roof of the pool house. I'm really sorry. Does she have another-"

He stopped abruptly as he caught sight of the television. Hank snatched up the remote again and turned it off, swearing under his breath as he did so.

"Floyd-"

"Why is your house on the news?" Floyd almost shrieked at Daven. "Is it because we're here?"

"Yes, they're out front right now," said Daven calmly, throwing a look at Hank that shut him up instantly. "Floyd, settle down, and look at me," Dav commanded in a surprisingly authoritative tone as he reached for the boy and took a hold of his wrists, clasping them to his own chest while walking over to the dining room table at the same time, all but dragging Floyd alongside him. Hank watched in fascination, far too surprised to say anything.

Daven held fast to Floyd as he sat. Floyd tried to wriggle away once and then stopped. "Breathe. Look at me. You're inside and they can't see through the walls. You're safe. Are you breathing? Steady."

"I can't." Floyd was on the very edge of a panic attack. "Why are they following us everywhere?"

"Because they make lots of money selling pictures of your famous dad," Daven answered matter-of-factly. "It's their job to take pictures. They aren't out to hurt anyone. It's a paycheck. Are you listening? You really need to steady your breathing or you're going to pass out."

"I don't know how," Floyd gasped after a moment, and Daven instantly moved his hands from Floyd's wrists to put one on his lower back, and one over his diaphragm, keeping him standing in place with a tight grip, at perfect eye level where he was sitting on the chair. Hank stood watching, frozen by the couch, remote still in hand.

"Concentrate. Count with me. Breathe in from deep down here (he patted his back) for four counts, then out for four from here (patting his belly)." Floyd tried, messed it up, then tried again. "Good. But you're still breathing too high. Take it lower. One more time. Stop looking at the television, it's off. Look at me. Now breathe in for five counts, and out for five. Okay, again and then we'll move on to six. Floyd, *stop* looking at the TV. Close your eyes."

The repeated this exercise for quite some time until they got to ten. To Hank's utter shock, his son was so deeply focused on his breathing tasks that he'd apparently forgotten about everything else around him. Daven had removed his hands after eight and let Floyd do the rest on his own.

After ten Daven stopped counting, and Floyd's eyes fluttered open and locked on to Dav. He did not look towards the television. Hank still dared not move for fear of breaking the spell, but his thoughts were racing in ten different directions.

Watching Floyd melt under Daven's calm ministrations vividly brought back the deep affection, admiration, and warmth for the man that Hank had been forcefully pushing out of his mind since the incident on Christmas day. There was absolutely no question that the next thing Hank was going to do was to let Daven know he was completely forgiven, and then ask for forgiveness in return. Beg, if needed.

Floyd broke the silence suddenly. He was perfectly calm. "Thank you. Are they still out there?"

Daven swallowed hard. "Probably. Let's find out. Hank, turn on the television again."

Hank nearly dropped the remote in his surprise. "Uh, no. Let's not do that."

"Turn it on," commanded Daven, and Hank only hesitated a second before complying. To his horror, there was the house, still...and the video was focusing on Avery sitting in his car, doing literally nothing of any interest whatsoever. Hank glanced anxiously at Floyd, who didn't seem perturbed at all. In fact, he seemed amused.

"Why are they looking at Avery? He's not even famous at all. I hope he doesn't pick his nose. Can you turn the sound on, dad?"

This was where Hank put his foot down. "No." He clicked off the television and threw a look at Dav that dared him to protest. "We're all going outside with Shannon. Together. We're going to walk right up to their cars, talk to them, get their names, be friendly, let them take pictures of us, and then we're going to come back and eat our cold burgers and melted shakes. Come on. Dav, harness up the dog."

"Uh, Hank...."

Hank went to front door and put on his coat, then held Floyd's out for him.

"Come on, Floyd. You can walk Shannon. Dav? Harness, now please."

Floyd walked over and let his dad put his coat on him. Since Dav was moving so slowly, Hank picked up the harness and slipped it onto Shannon, who was now carrying an enormous hot dog toy in her mouth. Hank opened the front door and stepped out, with Floyd close behind him.

"Dad, I don't like them. Why are we doing this?"

"Because I want them to stop harassing you and Theo, so we're going to be friendly and try to make peace. All I want you to do is come with me and just say hello. You don't have to do anything else. Can you do that?"

Floyd nodded, tightening his grip on Shannon's leash. Hank heard Dav come out behind him and laid a hand on his son's shoulder as they went down the porch stairs. "Okay. Just relax, buddy, we've got this. Just follow my lead."

Shannon immediately peed in the bushes, and Hank realized with a slight moment of panic that he hadn't brought a bag. Daven saw his expression. "She won't poop again yet. By the way, Hank, you are insane for doing this."

"Play along, Dav. We're on live television. Smile."

The trio - or quintet, rather, now that Avery and Lucas had scrambled to join them - crossed the street. Hank could feel, but not hear, the cameras clicking constantly as they went up to the lead car. He kept a hand tight on Floyd's shoulder when he thought he was about to bolt.

"Steady, Floyd," he murmured as he gestured for the man to roll down his window. The man did, but he looked confused and not a little scared.

"Good evening. I'm Hank, this is my son Floyd, and this is Daven. We noticed you're taking pictures of us, so we thought it was only proper to come say hello and introduce ourselves. How's your day been?"

"Uh....fine?" The man set his camera down on the passenger seat. "My name is Hank, too. What's the dog's name?"

"Shannon," answered Daven. "She's friendly," he added unnecessarily as Shannon stood up on her back legs and poked her head in the car while chomping down excitedly on her hot dog. The toy's squeaks practically drowned out what Hank said next.

"Look, you're welcome to take pictures of Daven and me, but I want to request that you stop following my sons around until they're famous on their own accord. I can't imagine you make too much money off of photos of them, do you?"

The other Hank was rendered a bit speechless. "Well, about $50 each, a couple times a month, maybe? Not too much."

"And how about my pictures?"

"A lot more," the man admitted nervously. "Hundreds."

Shannon dropped the toy in his lap, and he picked up the sloppy mess and handed it back to her with a disgusted look on his face. Hank smiled beatifically.

"Well, I will give you $1,500 to stop taking and selling pictures of my boys for an entire year. In return I'll invite you to a private event where you will make even more money off me. I trust you to honor our agreement at all times. Here's my card so you can contact me about receiving payment. Nice to meet you, and have a good day, sir. Floyd, come on. Take the toy away from her."

Dav was horrified as they walked to the next car. "Hank, what the hell? You can't pay off photographers like that! And giving them your cell number, too? What the hell are you doing?"

"Settle down, Dav. It's my secondary cell number that's always dead. Guess I need to find the charger now. Floyd, you doing okay?"

"Yeah."

They walked up to the next car repeated the process. That photographer congratulated Floyd warmly on getting his license, and told a funny story about his own daughter getting hers. They chatted for some time, and Floyd was delighted to pet his English Pointer that was now poking his head out of the rear window.

By the time they were to the fourth car, two more cars had rolled up. Hank hit all of them, and Hank again offered to pay them all off. Dav was still in shock and desperately trying to halt the proceedings, while Floyd was still extremely nervous and shy, but they did the best they could to get through it. Floyd even managed to have a full-on conversation with the last man, whose son he happened to know from school.

When they walked back to the house, Hank made them all turn around and wave to the cars before heading back inside.

Daven was visibly furious, but he kept his tone carefully in check. "Hey Floyd-o, do you mind me taking your dad away to talk to him for a minute? You can go ahead and eat without us."

Floyd was beaming and very visibly relaxed. "Sure. Can I use your microwave?"

"Of course. Hank? I would like to show you something in my office, please. It's rather urgent."

Hank had never seen Daven so angry before, and it was quite disorienting to be the one on the opposite end of the wrath that occasionally existed between them.

"Of all the stupid things you've ever done. Are you *trying* to get yourself jailed?"

"I didn't break any laws, Dav-"

"You most certainly did, and you know it. Bribery, for starters, and setting yourself up in the future for other accusations. Doing all of this on live television, to boot. What the hell are you thinking?"

Hank stayed calm despite the bitter novelty of being yelled at by his subordinate. "First of all, those live cameras have no microphones, so nobody besides us heard me. Secondly, I'm actually going to make them sign a contract before I pay them. All above board and legit. Then, I'm going to work on getting laws passed that prohibit photos of minors being sold for profit. So are you going to calm down, or are we going to have a problem here?"

"We already have a problem! You're totally out of your mind. All but one of those men work for the Urbanes, and you're actually going to literally sign a contract with them and allow them access to you that even our own photographers don't have? You are giving money to these vultures and actually trusting their word? Have you completely gone out of your senses?"

"Daven, that's enough," Hank warned.

"I agree with you there, Hank. This is definitely enough. I was already nervous about everything you've been up to lately, but I trusted you to at least have some common sense. This proves you don't, so I'm done. You'll have my resignation letter this evening by email, and by courier at the office tomorrow. I want you and Floyd to leave my house immediately."

Hank suddenly felt like the floor was collapsing beneath him. He could hardly breathe, and his chest began to burn fiercely. It seemed almost impossible to speak, but he managed somehow.

"Wait. Dav, please. You're blowing this out of proportion. At least let me explain. Floyd-"

"I don't want to hear it." Daven looked like he was about to throw a punch as he crossed around his desk and pulled the office door open.

Hank swallowed hard, feeling stinging in his eyes. He was *not* going to cry, no matter what.

"I'll go, but Dav...please don't kick Floyd out, too. He did nothing wrong." *God damn it,* he cussed at himself as a stray tear escaped before he could catch it.

"You both have to go," replied Dav, ice cold. "Also, don't even bother blocking my number again, because you'll never get another call from me."

"Okay. I'm sorry you're upset with me. I get it. But I did what I had to do for my son." He strode over to the window and yanked open the blinds. "Look."

Every single photographer's car was gone. Daven was unimpressed. "There will be more in five minutes. All you did was put a band-aid on a gunshot wound. Again, thank you for the food. Now if you don't mind, kindly let yourself out of the house for the last time and lock the door behind you. I'm going upstairs."

Hank didn't respond, he just watched him leave and then stood there a minute to collect himself before going back in the dining room to gather up his wallet and keys.

"Is Uncle Dav okay, dad?" Floyd said between bites of his burger.

"I think so. Where'd he go?"

"Said he had to go upstairs for a while."

Hank cleared his throat. "I think Dav isn't feeling well but he doesn't want to admit it to us. What would you think if we just went ahead and let him rest? I'll clean up all this trash while you finish your burger."

Floyd seemed disappointed, but he didn't argue. Hank carefully picked up every piece of trash and threw it all into the composter, including Daven's uneaten southwest burger and onion rings. Then he drained the root beer float mush into the sink, cleaned the sink, and took off Shannon's harness to hang it up in the closet. The remote needed to go back on top of the television, so he did that, too.

The house was perfectly spotless now. Everything was done. No need to stick around anymore.

"Okay. Say goodbye to Shannon, and let's head out."

Floyd stood up and threw his wrappers in the trash.

"Hey, Floyd?" asked Hank, still feeling in total shock by what had just happened with Dav. "I'm so very proud of you for how you handled those photographers. You did good. Thanks, kiddo."

"Sure, dad. It wasn't as bad as I thought. They were nice. Except for the third guy."

Hank smiled a little. "Yeah, he's a pain in the ass. But he won't follow you anymore. None of them will."

Floyd didn't seemed wholly convinced. "There are so many more, though."

"Then I better start working on them, too. Come on, let's go."

Hank couldn't help but feel an enormous sense of loss as he looked around Daven's house for the very last time. Floyd went out first and headed straight to the car, leaving Hank standing in the entryway. He shut off the light, then heard Dav coming down the stairs.

Against every instinct he had to flee and follow Floyd into the SUV, he turned the light back on and waited with heart pounding.

Daven turned the corner, stopping in surprise at seeing him still standing there.

"Did you forget something?" he asked in a totally normal tone, as if he was asking for the time. He had changed into his running clothes and was clearly on the way to the gym downstairs.

"Yeah. I mean, no. Sorry, I'm right now, kind of having a hard time believing this is happening."

"Please leave your copy of my house key on that sideboard," Daven said calmly, nodding to the piece of furniture in question. Without further adieu, he turned and went down the stairs to his basement. Hank stood there frozen for a few moments, then removed the key in question from his keychain and set it down with a soft metallic sound. He couldn't bear to look around the house one more time, so he closed his eyes as he shut the lights off and locked the door behind him.

He opened his eyes to the sight of seven more press cars lined up across the street, exactly as Daven had predicted.

CHAPTER FOUR

Bancroft Manor

Same day

It seemed to Floyd that an eternity or two had gone by in the spare room while he waited his turn for a reckoning, stomach twisting into several varieties of knots the entire time. Surely Theo wasn't getting it *that* bad? They must have been talking a lot, that's all. Hopefully lots and lots of talking. Or maybe his dad just wanted him to suffer, since he knew how much waiting like this tormented his oldest son.

He pulled his jacket tighter and shivered again, then sat on the bed and pulled the heavy blanket around him like a protective barrier and wedged himself against the headboard. He didn't move when his father finally appeared half an hour later and led the still-sniffling Theo to a corner. When Hank looked at him and jerked his head toward the door, Floyd silently rose, folded the blanket back up, and trudged behind him to the study.

"Hey. Sorry it took so long. Theo had a really hard time getting through it."

Oh god. Floyd glanced at the clock and was astonished to see only 45 minutes had passed since he was last in this room.

Hank continued, "I went really easy on him, don't worry. He was just very emotional about the whole thing and needed a lot of time to settle down and talk. He's very worried about you, you know."

Floyd swallowed hard, but said nothing.

"Relax, son. You've got yourself all wound up because you've been waiting, that's all. If I'd known he was going to take so long, you would have been up first. Anything you'd like to say?"

Floyd's tongue felt very thick all of a sudden. "I'm sorry. For everything I did and said today, and…"

"I know. It's okay. The only thing you're being punished for is fighting with Theo in the car and not being honest with Avery, so let's get this over with. If you promise me you'll behave, I'll go easy on you, too."

Floyd nodded, and walked up to the desk to take position. "I promise, dad. Thank you."

After it was done, Hank took Floyd back to the spare room and dropped him off at the opposite corner from Theo with a reassuring squeeze on his shoulder.

"I'll be back in an hour. You know the rules. No talking, no fidgeting."

Two minutes later, Theo tentatively asked from his corner if Floyd was okay.

Floyd's nerves prickled instantly, his irritation at Theody's unflattering description of his panic attack rushing to the forefront again.

"I'm fine, Theody. Heard you were acting like a little bitch, though. What a surprise."

Theo did not rise to the bait. "I'm glad you're okay."

"Yeah? Well I don't care what you think, so shut up and go break another sculpture."

Silence.

Ten seconds later the door opened and Floyd was unceremoniously yanked out of the corner by his very angry father.

"Alright. I've officially had it with you. Come on."

"Dad!" Floyd pleaded in shock as he was bodily pulled down the hall to Hank's study. "What are you doing?"

"You don't remember that I can monitor every room in the house? Really? How dare you make such a vicious comment to your brother at a time like this."

Oh, shit. "I'm so sorry, dad. I have-"

"Pants down and hands on the desk. Now."

Floyd's entire body went numb in a flash. His dad had never believed in spanking on the bare, although Theody got it once when he was eight for starting a fire in the backyard that took out several hedges and a lemon tree. The memory of the trauma his brother suffered on that awful day had haunted Floyd ever since.

Hank took off his belt as he spoke with the deadly calm that indicated he was moments away from exploding. Floyd backed away towards the door.

"*Floyd*. Don't make it worse for yourself."

"Worse?" he cried. "How could I possibly make this worse?"

Everyone hates me, Hank moped as he made himself some tea in the kitchen after returning the inconsolable Floyd to the spare room. Maybe Taylor didn't hate him, or a few people at the office, but there was far more to life than work friends. There also wasn't much to life at all without Daven. The thought of going even one full day with him as an enemy was too much to bear.

So Hank drank his tea, ate a Moon Pie, then took a shot of whiskey and prepared himself for a fight. Daven's phone rang only once, so Hank hung up and tried again, thinking it was a bad connection. This time, it didn't ring at all and went to a generic recording. The third time, too. Puzzled, he started to dial a fourth time, then stopped.

Daven had blocked his number. The realization hit him like the old cliché of stepping on a rake and getting smacked in the face. In disbelief he went to Floyd's room and called him from his son's cell. Certainly Uncle Dav wouldn't block Floyd-o, too?

"We're sorry. Your call cannot be completed to this number. Goodbye."

Then he tried from Theo's phone, and then Avery's, and then the house's landline. All of them were blocked.

Fuck...

He went back to his study and pulled up the live feed from the spare room to check on Floyd. The boys were talking again.

"...wasn't your fault. I'm so sorry, Theody. Are you even listening?"

"Yeah."

"You forgive me?"

"Yeah, but only if you shut up so we don't get in trouble again."

Floyd left his corner and went to lay down on the bed - on his stomach, naturally - and started to sob again. Hank got up and activated the intercom switch on the wall, keeping his eyes on the video feed.

"I'm giving you ten seconds to get back in the corner. Ten. Nine. Eight."

Floyd rose up and dragged himself back into place.

"Thank you."

Hank slammed down the intercom switch, sighed heavily and rubbed his temples for a few minutes. He then called Rupert, feeling absurdly relieved when he actually picked up.

"Hey, Rupe. Got a minute? Or thirty?"

"I'm in the middle of dinner, but I can talk for a few minutes. What's up, boss?"

"Great, thanks. It's been a day, man. I can't even tell you. Have you spoken to Daven recently, by chance?"

"No, I haven't spoken to him today."

"Okay, well...I'm not going to beat around the bush, so here goes. Daven is quitting because of me. I could really use your advice on how to change his mind."

Rupert nodded. "Oh, I see. Honestly, Hank, this isn't the best time or place for that kind of conversation. Can I call you in about an hour, maybe around 9pm?"

Hank tried not to let the disappointment come through in his tone. "Yeah, of course. I'll be up."

He then impulsively called Lucas, even knowing it could easily lead to another fight with Daven if he wasn't careful.

"Hey, are you with Daven?" he asked as casually as he could manage.

"Yes, sir, as ordered."

"Good. Where are you guys?"

"Yamashiro, but we're leaving shortly. He's just now paying the bill."

"Okay, thanks. I just wanted to make sure he's alright, since I haven't heard back from him regarding something urgent we had discussed today."

Lucas said quickly, "Sir, I don't know if you will hear back, to be honest. He's drunk."

Hank thought he hadn't heard correctly. "He's...he's what?"

"Drunk. *Really* drunk, actually. He told me not to take any calls from you, but you're the boss, so I picked up anyway."

"Yeah, good choice. Thanks Lucas. Who are you guys with?" It was a highly inappropriate question, and they both knew it. Lucas had every right not to answer, and Hank was about to take it back before his guard answered anyway.

"Rupert and his family, and some of their friends from out of town."

Rupert and his family.

Rupert, who just told him less than ten minutes ago that he hadn't spoken to Dav today.

Rupert.... lied to him.

Hank felt like an arrow had been shot through his chest.

"Okay, great. That's good, I guess. Just get Dav home safely, then. I won't tell him we spoke, of course. Talk to you tomorrow."

He left his study and went straight to his bedroom, shutting his phone completely off and quietly locking the door behind him.

He forgot all about the boys, who were still obediently standing in their corners when he raced back to the spare room more than three hours later to release them.

CHAPTER FIVE

Tuesday, January 11

For the first time in his life, Hank called out sick from work when he wasn't actually sick. It was 8:00am and the boys were eating breakfast when he finally got dressed and ventured down the stairs.

Theo was startled to see him, and so was the chef, who quickly whipped up another plate for his boss. He took it gratefully and sat down at the table across from Theo.

"Dad? Why aren't you at work? Are you alright?"

"I'm fine, Theody. Working from home today to catch up on some projects."

"Oh."

Hank was determined to eat his meal in silence, but Theo had other ideas.

"Are you and Uncle Dav really fighting, dad?" Theo asked, and Hank nearly choked on his sausage as he eyed Floyd, who looked sheepishly down at his eggs.

"None of your business," he replied sternly.

Theo looked like he was about to cry. "Sorry, was just trying to make conversation. Your phone's ringing."

Stewart was calling. Hank sent it to voicemail. Just as he did that, he noticed a new email notification from Rupert. Unable to resist temptation, he clicked on it even though he knew he'd regret it.

"Hank, what's going on? I waited all night for you to call me back last night. Where are you this morning? Thanks - Rupe."

Hank deleted it, then scrolled backwards through his emails while his heart pounded like a bass drum. Surprisingly, the promised resignation letter from Daven was nowhere to be found. He scrolled through three times just to make sure.

Nothing. What the hell did *that* mean?

"Theo, run up to my sitting room and see if Daven's truck is in his driveway."

The boy complied instantly, and Hank waited for his footsteps to fade before he set his fork down and looked at Floyd.

"What did you tell Theo, exactly? Be honest. I'm not mad."

"That I tried to call Uncle Dav last night but he blocked my phone," Floyd responded quietly, eyes on his plate. "The house phone is blocked, too. And Theo's cell."

"I know. I'm sorry."

"What did you do?" Floyd looked absolutely devastated.

Hank was at least glad the poor kid wasn't blaming himself, but there was very little he could say to make this any better. "Can't say, but I'm working on a resolution. Please be patient."

"What about Rupert? When you are going to ask if Theo and I can home school with his kids? The new semester starts next week."

Oh god....

Theo ran back down the stairs, thankfully saving Hank from having to answer that question. "Dad! Dad!!!"

"What the hell, Theo?"

"Shannon's loose! I just saw her run down the street all by herself! Where's Uncle Dav?"

"Fuck," blurted Hank, and he and Floyd jumped up and ran to front door, with Theo close behind. Sure enough, Shannon was racing down the middle of the street with her leash in her mouth, looking as gleefully joyous and wild as any dog had ever looked. All three of them ran out to catch her, but she dodged them and kept going straight towards Olympic Blvd.

"Boys, back in the house. Now."

Hank jumped into the Thunderbird without a second thought and roared down the street by himself, which he took a moment to appreciate. It was nice to not have guards and drivers clinging to him hand and foot. He picked up the phone and called Avery.

"Hey. Take an SUV down to Olympic and go...right. I'll go left. Daven's dog is on the loose and we're trying to catch her. Yes, I'm by myself. Hurry. Got to go."

Hank drove around for almost two hours with absolutely no sign of Shannon. His phone had long died, so he had almost given up until he turned into a park and saw three adults trying to corner her on a playground. The Thunderbird roared to a stop at the foot of the swings and he jumped out.

"Shannon, come here, baby girl! Come on."

Shannon spied him, and with a burst of energy she snatched up a tennis ball from the ground and ran straight at him. He yanked onto her harness and held on for dear life. It promptly snapped in his hands, and she almost got away again before he grabbed her by the tail and wrapped a strong arm around her torso. The three ladies were clinging on to each other now, staring at him in awe.

"Hank Bancroft! Oh my goodness!" they exclaimed happily. Hank ignored them long enough to get Shannon in the car (making sure all the windows were rolled up and the back doors locked so she couldn't escape again). Then he went over to them and shook their hands.

"Thank you so much, ladies. Thank you very much. We would have been devastated to lose her. I really appreciate your help."

One of the ladies had a camera, so Hank obliged them by taking photos with each of them, and then the three of them wanted a picture with Shannon, and then with the infamous Thunderbird, too. He was desperate to get Dav's baby back to him after secretly enjoying feeling like a total rock star for a few minutes, and was relieved when they finally let him go.

A black SUV had pulled up behind him during the photo shoot. Avery and his sons, of course. Hank waved at them and then got in the car and headed for home, taking different side streets than usual because he wasn't sure exactly how to get to Daven's house from the park, and Avery honked at him when he took a wrong turn. He quickly flipped a u-turn and went the other way, when suddenly he spotted Daven across the street, climbing down a slope at a different park with Lucas a few feet behind him.

Hank pulled another U-turn, got honked at again by Avery, but ignored it and smoothly raced up an alley alongside the park to intercept the men.

Dav heard the Thunderbird and stopped in surprise as Hank glided up next to him and rolled down the window. "I've got Shannon, she's fine. Hop in and I'll drive you guys home."

Daven crossed in front of the car and leaned in the passenger side to reach back towards Shannon. She dropped the tennis ball into the front seat and barked happily at him, then whined while he rubbed her ears and cooed at her.

"Hank, I can't thank you enough. I don't know what to say. I'll walk her home from here, can you unlock the door?"

"Well, no...her harness snapped into pieces when I grabbed her, and I don't know where her leash went. For an older dog, she's really strong."

"Yes. Do you have a spare leash in the trunk?"

He knew there were a few back there. Maybe three, plus a harness or two. "No, sorry. You can ride with me, or with Avery if you prefer."

"I'll ride with Avery. Thank you, Hank, so much. If you can just wait in the car for a minute when we get there, I'll grab her other harness."

"Yeah, of course."

Hank watched Daven climb in the SUV and felt his heart break almost as much as it had yesterday. He waved to let Avery pull in front of him and lead the way back to Daven's house. When they arrived, Daven harnessed Shannon in the backseat and took her inside with the boys and Avery, who were all delighted at the outcome of the chase. Hank knew he should leave, but Daven's truck blocked him from moving forward in the driveway and Avery's SUV blocked him from backing out of it. Apparently he was expected to awkwardly wait in the car for everyone to decide the reunion was over.

And awkward, it was. Very. After a minute or two with no guard or sons in sight, he got out of the car and went to the front door. Daven let him in without comment.

"Sorry Dav, we'll get going. Floyd, Theo, Avery. Everyone out. Back to the house." Then, quietly but sternly to his favorite guard: "You should have already been outside with me."

"Sorry, boss, I actually thought you were coming in. I guess this makes us even for you taking off on me all alone two hours ago."

Hank fixed him with a ferocious glare. "Do you *really* think it's wise to get smart with me right now?" he snapped, still keeping his voice low.

Avery stepped back a little, startled at Hank's unexpected reaction to what was intended to be a lighthearted remark. "Sir, I....I'm sorry. I wasn't trying to...forgive me."

Hank nodded and reluctantly let it drop. He would have docked a full day's pay for any other guard who left him unguarded for any amount of time, never mind one who talked back to him like that, but he had put poor Avery through enough shit lately. It wasn't his fault Hank's life was miserable at the moment.

Everyone in his group suddenly departed at the same time, which left Hank face to face to Daven at the door. He didn't want to lose what might be his only chance to say something.

"I thought you were going to send me an email last night," he blurted quickly.

Daven ignored the remark completely and scooted past him through the doorway, then waved again at the boys and Avery as they got in the SUV. "Thanks guys. I owe you. Let me pull the truck out of the way for you."

Dav climbed into his truck as Hank just stood there, somewhat dumbfounded and numb. He quickly came to his senses and got in the Thunderbird, resisting the urge to angrily gun it across the perfect front lawn like Floyd had done a couple weeks ago. He would never do it, but had to admit that it would be an incredibly satisfying experience right about now.

He even found himself briefly envying his son for knowing exactly how it felt.

When Hank got home he plugged his phone in at his desk and realized with a start that it was almost 10:30am. He had missed his daily call with Harmon. Sure enough, there were three missed calls on his cell. But no messages from him; just one from Stewart.

First things first, however. He hit the intercom button that connected to the security offices.

"Avery, report to my study on the double."

There was a longer pause than usual, then Avery's voice. "Yes, sir, on my way."

Less than a minute later the very subdued head of security arrived. He'd been reprimanded by Hank several times before for various minor breaches of policy, usually related to paperwork delays, but this was different. It was emotional, very personal. For that reason, Avery was incredibly nervous.

"Hey," said Hank quickly as he rose and came around to the front of his desk to lean against it.

"Boss, I'm so very-"

"Correct, I'm the boss, so I'll do the talking. I owe you a seriously huge apology for the way I snapped at you. You didn't deserve it. I mean, nobody does, but especially not *you*. I'm a fucking idiot, and I'm really sorry. Wish I could take it back."

"Uh...well, thank you, sir, but you were right about me leaving you alone like that."

"Yes I was, and I expect that to never happen again."

Avery swallowed hard. "It won't. And with respect, I fully expect you not to take off without a guard again, either. Especially with a dead cell phone. It nearly gave me a stroke trying to find you."

"Deal. Sorry." Hank reached out to shake his hand, and then patted him on the back as he walked him out. "Keep up the good work. I really need you more than ever right now."

Hank shut the door behind him, then raced back to his phone before Stewart could slap his hands for not keeping to the call schedule. Then again, maybe that's what the voicemail was for. He didn't want to know.

"Harmon, fuck, I'm so sorry. You wouldn't believe what I've been doing for the past two hours."

"Let me guess. Chasing Daven's loose dog all around the city and catching him yourself at the park? You're a true hero, Mr. Bancroft."

"Wait…what?" Hank stuttered, alarm prickling the hairs at the back of his neck. "How the *hell* did you know that?"

Harmon paused dramatically. "It was all over the news. There was a live feed of the pursuit, even aired here in Denver. Quite entertaining. You didn't know?"

Hank forced himself to breathe deeply in order to clear away the sudden dizziness. *Fuck.* This was getting out of hand.

"Please tell me you're joking. Because I won't be able to go out in public any more after this."

Harmon paused again, and then laughed. "I'm sorry, Hank. Just messing with you. No, a young lady who took a picture with you sent the story into the newswire a few minutes ago and one of our Denver reporters forwarded it to a few of us. She thought it was cute. You *are* a hero, you know."

"I'm...holy shit. You are a *horrible* person." Relief washed over him like a waterfall, and against his will Hank found himself grinning at the absurd imagery of the whole fiasco being broadcast live. "You got me good, I admit it. Thanks for the heart attack. Jesus H Christ on a pogo stick."

Harmon cleared his throat. "Yeah. Speaking of heart attacks, I got a call from Stewart on Friday. Why did you tell him that I asked you to say Janet wasn't a double agent?"

"Because I don't want to lose my fucking job, that's why," Hank retorted defensively, all amusement over the dog chase instantly forgotten. "You should have never asked me that."

"I asked you for a reason. You know how these things can be sometimes."

"No, I don't know. Because I don't play games."

Yeah...so says the chess grand master. "Fine. Then I'm going to be perfectly upfront. We know Janet was double, and we figured out what you're up to as far as trying to frame me for her murder. I was trying to get Colbert to-"

Hank felt like screaming all of a sudden. "*Frame?* It's not *framing* when you're actually guilty, Harmon. The truth will come out soon enough."

"No it won't. Haven't you read the FBI message this morning?"

Hank turned to his computer and quickly pulled up his email. "No. I've been a little busy playing reverse Lassie all morning with my chief of staff. Hang on."

It was a press release blurb that had been sent to both parties in advance of an afternoon release:

After reviewing all video footage available, as well as extensive forensic testing, we are unable to draw any clues as to the identity of the murderer. Ms. Janet died from a gunshot wound to the head with an untraceable bullet. The case is now considered on hold until new evidence arises.

"You have got to be fucking kidding me," Hank said out loud, feeling his headache arising anew at the back of his head.

"No one is fucking kidding you. That was the FBI's determination, which you *know* I could not possibly influence."

"Even so, you got away with it. Congratulations," Hank offered bitterly.

"Hank, please. If you want to formally accuse me, do so. I'll be happy to prove it wasn't us. But I, for one, would prefer that this incident to be the last one in which we are foes. Think about it. We believe in a lot of the same things, and if our parties unite on those fronts there's nothing that can stop us. We can still fight about the shit we disagree on, because that's our job, but-"

"Wait, what? Are you on drugs?" Hank laughed out loud, not able to believe what he was hearing.

"No. I knew you were going to say that. Actually, I want to meet with you in person this Friday. You and me. Talk some shit out. We can't keep going like this. You know that, right?"

Sounds like every single one of my conversations with Floyd lately, Hank thought wryly.

"Yeah, I've...I know. I hear you, and I don't want to fight either. But Harmon, you can't be serious. You know I don't trust you as far as I can throw you."

Harmon cleared his throat again. "If you prefer, the three of us can meet to talk. I know Daven is not a fan of mine, but his objectivity would be useful to both of us. Perhaps you should ask him for his opinion on this."

Hank laughed again. "Holy shit. You are definitely on drugs if you think Dav is going to go for this. Can I have some of what you're having?"

There was a long pause from the other end of the line.

"I'm trying to make peace, Hank."

"But I'm not. Go fuck yourself."

Hank hung up and reached into his refrigerator for a bottle of whiskey. His phone rang almost immediately, and it was Harmon. Of course. Knowing that Stewart would slap his hand for not obeying the ten-minute rule, Hank reluctantly picked up.

"What now?"

"We still have five minutes, Hank."

"Okay, I'll sing you a song. What would you like to hear? Maybe *I Want to Hold Your Hand* by the Beatles?"

"Stop fucking with me, Hank. I just want you to ask Daven if he thinks it's a good idea for us to meet. That's all. Start small. If he says no, I'll drop it."

Hank looked at the bottle of whiskey, but did not touch it. He felt severely depressed all of a sudden. "Yeah, well. I would, but we're not exactly on speaking terms right now."

"Oh." Harmon sounded puzzled rather than pleased, which was definitely a change. "Well, then we finally have something in common. I'm not speaking to Colbert at the moment, either."

Hank sat up straighter, now highly invested in this surreal conversation. Harmon and Colbert were thick as thieves, probably closer than even Hank and Dav. "Why are you telling me this? And why did I tell you that about me and Dav? I must be on drugs, too."

Harmon actually chuckled a little at that. "Please be serious, Hank. I know you don't believe anything I say, but I would bet my life on anything you say. Your transparency is truly self-destructive. You should channel that trait into other things. Like cooperation with my party on issues that matter to all of us."

"You aren't kidding about the self-destructive part. What did Colbert do?" asked Hank, genuinely curious now, and all but forgetting he was speaking intimately to the person he hated most in the world.

"Ah, well. Let's just say it's a personality issue. What did Daven do?"

"He didn't do anything. I did. Also a personality issue. Wait, what the fuck? *Why* am I even talking to you about this?"

"Because it's lonely at the top, Hank. And we're as 'top' as it gets. So..."

Yeah, tell me about it...you have no fucking idea how lonely I am right now.

Hank felt his guard lowering even further, and for once he didn't fight it. "Okay, so...you must realize I'm seriously doubting your motives are pure, right?"

86

Harmon cleared his throat, and now his tone was full of irritation. "Okay, Hank. Let's get real. You want to talk about pure motives? Let's take a look at how many times the great Hank Bancroft has totally screwed me over personally in the past few years in order to advance his own agenda. How much time do you have? Because we're definitely going to need more than ten minutes."

"I haven't-"

"You are a master of manipulation and domination, but you mask it all behind this facade of honesty and purity. And you do hide it well, I must admit. A great talent, light years ahead of me. So I guarantee you that I have far more reason to suspect your motives than you'll ever have to suspect mine."

Hank was actually taken aback by this attack. Not that it wasn't anything he didn't already know...just that he didn't know anyone else knew it.

"The difference between us, Harmon, is that I use my *talents* towards the greater good. You only care about yourself. And that's why I don't trust you. Are we done now?"

"It appears we have reached an impasse, so yes, I'm done. I still have one request. Don't tell anyone I'm having issues with

Colbert. I shared that with you willingly in order to open a dialogue. Obviously I'm regretting it now, but what's said is said."

"No need. I won't tell anyone." Hank was actually surprised to realize he meant that. "I would say I trust you not to say anything about me and Daven either, but that would be a lie. I fully expect to see it on the front page tomorrow."

"You won't. I'm sure your boys destroying priceless art at the library is a far more interesting story, anyway."

Hank closed his eyes and took a deep breath. "It wasn't anywhere close to priceless, and I have the receipt to prove it. God. The shit we have to put up with from the paparazzi."

"Yeah. I can't wait for the news of my colonoscopy tomorrow to hit the wires. Look, this may not have been the most pleasant discussion, but I'm still glad we had it anyway. Thank you for your time. Shall we say 10am tomorrow for more pointless bickering, Hank?"

There was a very long pause while Hank looked at the newspaper on his desk that featured a photo of him and Daven cutting a ribbon together at the new container port in San Pedro a few weeks back that was opening today. They were both smiling. Happy. Unaware of the impending disaster that was about to split them apart at the seams.

With equal amounts of hesitation and determination, Hank made the first of many decisions he would come to deeply regret in just four months' time.

"I'll meet with you Friday, but not in Denver. Wheels down in Las Vegas at 9am. I'll pick the meeting place and we'll ride there together with my own guards and driver. That's the *only* way I'm agreeing to it. And you have my word there will be absolutely no tricks or games."

"I'm not happy with those terms, to be honest. But I'll do it," Harmon said in an annoyed tone.

"Good. Since it was your idea, I'll leave it up to you to clear it through Stewart. Let me know what he says so I can make the arrangements."

CHAPTER SIX

Tuesday, Jan 11 - continued

Seditionists HQ

(Rupert's first day back at work)

Taylor sat slumped in a booth in the cafeteria and pecked at her laptop listlessly, only intensifying her activity with a burst of energy as Rupert appeared in the doorway and walked up to stand at her table. So much for trying to deter him from bothering her.

"Late lunch, huh?" he remarked with as small smile. "Got a minute?"

"4pm is still technically not dinner, so yes...lunch. I'm assuming this convo is appropriate for a public space?"

He looked around with his eyebrows furrowed. "There's...nobody here, Taylor. Heard from Hank yet?"

"Not since he told me he wasn't coming in. You?"

"No. I'm on his shit list again, so..."

"Why?" asked Taylor curiously, softening her attitude towards him a bit. "You said everything was fine yesterday."

"It was. But...my first day back, and I haven't heard a peep from him? And my phone is still blocked. He hasn't answered my email. I wanted to tell him what happened last night with Daven before he hears it from Lucas. But I think he already has. In that case, I'm toast."

"One second," Taylor interrupted as she pulled out her ringing cell. It was Hank, but she didn't want Rupert to know, so she cleared her throat and pitched her voice up cheerfully. "Good afternoon, this is Taylor. How may I help you?"

"Taylor?"

"Yes?"

"Doesn't sound like you. I'm guessing you have company. Hey, listen. I'm expecting a FedEx or UPS letter. Just wondering if it came."

"Not yet. Who is it from so I can keep an eye out?"

"Umm. Daven. No one else should be allowed to see it. Isn't the last FedEx at like 7pm?"

"No, 4:30. I'll check and let you know."

"Thanks kiddo. Just so you know, I haven't spoken to Rupert yet, and I'm not ready to."

"Yes, I figured that out. Thank you."

"Call me back after 4:30."

Taylor hung up, carefully set her drink aside and closed the lid to her laptop, then motioned for Rupert to sit down with her. "Okay, I'll bite. What happened last night with Daven?"

Bancroft Manor

For what seemed like the tenth time, Hank erased his email to Daven and started all over again. He had been composing it for almost two hours, and nothing sounded right. It was either too pandering, too desperate, or too cold. So after hanging up Taylor, he decided to go for a walk and went downstairs to the security office to find Avery, and was quite surprised to see

Floyd chatted animatedly with Brittany at her desk. He wasn't allowed downstairs, and everyone knew it.

"Hey," he said mildly to Floyd, not wanting Brittany to feel uncomfortable. "When did you get back from the animal shelter? I didn't hear the front door chime."

"Maybe 15 minutes ago, sir," he replied, a little shakily. "Theo is still at the beach clean-up."

Hank nodded. "Okay. Go wait for me in my study."

Floyd's eyes went wide, but he complied without hesitation. Hank then looked at Brittany, who stood up, calm as ever.

"Sir, he was just-"

"Next time he comes down here, you send him back up immediately or I'll want to know the reason why. Are we clear? I've told you this before."

She seemed to take on a sudden defensive posture, and Hank picked up on it immediately and cut her off before she could argue.

"I don't want to hear anything but yes or no," Hank said sternly.

"Yes, sir. But-"

Hank bristled and was just about to bark something at her when Avery walked in, obviously not realizing he would be interrupting anything.

"My apologies, boss," he said, immediately turning to go back out.

"No problem, we're done here." Hank did not look at Brittany again as he left the office. Whatever he had been about to say would have done more harm than good, anyway. Theo was at the top of the stairs when he was on his way back to Floyd.

"How was the beach clean-up, Theody?"

"Good. But I got sunburned."

"In January? Got to love California. Go get cleaned up and rest. Dinner in 90 minutes."

Floyd was fidgeting madly as Hank entered the study and shut the door, immediately speaking as he walked around his oldest and sat down in his chair.

"You know the rule about going down into the basement. Tell me why you broke it."

"I didn't know you'd come downstairs at the same time."

Hank sighed. "Floyd, that's not the point, and that was a piss poor job of avoiding the question. I don't understand why you can't just behave yourself and not break rules. It's simple. Can you explain to me what I'm missing?"

"Yes, sir. You're missing Brittany's birthday." He held up a pink envelope. "Theody and I got her a card and I was about to give it to her. We signed it for you, too, because we knew you'd forget."

Hank felt like throwing himself down the nearest laundry chute. *What an ass, Hank. Good job.*

He collected himself quickly. "You were correct, I forgot. Thank you. But you can't just choose when to obey rules or not. You did the wrong thing, for the right reasons. But it's still wrong. Next time ask me. I would have said yes to this."

"Yes, sir. I'm sorry," Floyd responded politely.

Hank eyed him carefully, sensing something he didn't really like. "Are you feeling okay?"

Other than not being able to sit down for the past 18 hours, you mean?

Hank's phone rang before Floyd could respond, and he went to dig it out of his pocket. "Hang on, Floyd. Yes, Taylor?"

FedEx and UPS just came and there's nothing from the person you're waiting for. But something else did come, and you're not going to like it. I'm in your office with the door closed.

"Jesus Christ, I don't know if I want to hear this. Okay...what now?"

We just received by courier a subpoena from Stewart at the FBI. You have to turn over your phone records for the entire month of December.

"Mine? Like, *mine* , personally?"

Yes, sir. Home, office, cell. Within seven days.

Hank was not exactly stunned by this turn of events, considering everything that had happened in December. He was more curious than anything else, but his conscious was clear enough to keep him from being too alarmed.

"Alright. I'll get on it tomorrow morning with Shane. Thanks, Taylor. See you then."

He turned back to Floyd. "Okay, we're done here. I need to make some calls."

Floyd held up the envelope again. "Sir, may I please take this downstairs to Brittany?"

"That's exactly what you should have done in the first place - ask me. Yes. Go on, I'll see you at dinner."

Floyd went, secretly glad for Taylor having interrupted his dad's anger towards him and redirecting it somewhere else entirely.

Hank hit the intercom to Brittany's office to tell her he was sending Floyd down, then picked up the phone to check the hours-old voicemail from Stewart.

Hank, this is Stewart in Philadelphia. You're going to be getting a subpoena from me today in regards to your phone records for December. This is basically just to continue the investigation on Janet, which I need to discuss with you in more depth. I also need to take a statement from you regarding a deal you allegedly made some photographers yesterday. Hoping you can come to Philadelphia on Friday morning. Call me back at your earliest convenience.

Fuck.

"Hoping you can come" really meant *"if you don't come, your ass is grass."* He was supposed to meet with Harmon on Friday in Las Vegas, and this message was almost ten hours old. He cursed at himself for ignoring it earlier, because now it was almost 8pm in Philadelphia. He dialed Harmon instead.

"Hey. Did you hear back from Stewart about us meeting in Vegas on Friday?"

"Yes, but he said no. I was going to talk to you about it tomorrow on our call."

"Did he say why?"

"No, he was very evasive about the whole thing. I'm in a meeting. Can we talk tomorrow?"

"Yeah, sorry. Bye."

There was another new email notification from Rupert. He set the phone down, then turned to his computer and opened it up.

Hank - we really need to talk. Last night would have been better. Please call me tonight at your convenience. Anytime is fine. Thanks, Rupe

Hank rapidly tapped back a snippy reply:

I'm not available. I hope you enjoyed your dinner at Yamashiro last night. I'm certain Daven did, too. Thanks, Hank

Then he started a new email to Daven:

I did not receive your email last night, or your letter today. Please let me know if you've changed your mind. Thanks, Hank.

Just before he was about to end the work day, he noticed an email from Stewart that he had missed, although it came in two hours ago.

Hank - not sure if you got my voicemail from this morning. Let me know.

This was why being distracted by a runaway dog was never a good thing....

Stewart, I just picked it up. Sorry. I've been out of pocket most of the day due to illness. I will be there on Friday morning. What time? Thanks, Hank

Then he reached down and turned his computer completely off, skipping the shut down process. He knew that would wreak havoc upon booting up next time, but he didn't care. It would be just another irritation in a shitload of irritations for the week.

CPSIA information can be obtained
at www.ICGtesting.com
Printed in the USA
BVHW091503140621
609529BV00007B/2003